An Octopus Named MOM

Written by Kathleen Flaherty   Illustrated by Jennifer Caulfield Donehey

three
bean press

Biographies

Kathleen Marion Flaherty

Kathleen lives in Millis, Massachusetts, with her husband and their four children. She is a graduate of Johnson and Wales University and has worked with children for over 17 years. Kathleen grew up spending her summers on Hog Island, Rhode Island, and now continues that tradition with her family where she enjoys boating, gardening, writing, reading, and cooking. She uses the island as a classroom to teach her children to be one with nature.

Jennifer Caulfield Donehey

Jennifer studied art at Westfield State College and Massachusetts College of Art, with a concentration in illustration and drawing. Working primarily in watercolor and acrylics, Jennifer is adept at capturing a range of subjects, from food illustrations as a chalkboard artist and muralist for Roche Bros.' chain of grocery stores to commissioned pet portraits to characters and settings in children's books. Jennifer loves cooking, hiking, and landscaping (she even created her home's 15' x 30' bluestone mosaic patio, shown here). She lives in Millis, Massachusetts, with her husband, two children, and black lab, and she enjoys getaways to their cabin in Vermont.

An Octopus Named Mom
Published by:
Three Bean Press, LLC
P.O. Box 301711
Jamaica Plain, MA 02130
info@threebeanpress.com • www.threebeanpress.com

Text copyright © 2012 by Kathleen Flaherty
Illustrations copyright © 2012 by Jennifer Caulfield Donehey

Publishers Cataloging-in-Publication Data
Flaherty, Kathleen
An Octopus Named Mom / by Kathleen Flaherty.
p. cm.
Summary: A young boy wishes for his mom to become an octopus so that she has more time for him.
But is this really a wish he wants to come true?

ISBN 978-0-9767276-8-2
[1. Children—Fiction. 2. Wishes—Fiction. 3. Octopus—Fiction. 4. Moms—Fiction.]
I. Donehey, Jennifer Caulfield, Ill. II. Title.

LCCN 2012939499

Printed in the United States through Four Colour Print Group, Louisville, KY.
10 9 8 7 6 5 4 3 2 1

For more information about *An Octopus Named Mom* and to inquire about school visits, go to www.octopusnamedmom.com.

Dedication

To my mother, Loretta: You dedicated your life to your five children and shared your love and time with each one of us. You exhibited the art of multitasking with poise and grace. I thank you and dedicate this book in memory of you.

And for Rob, Lydia, Bridget, Braeden, and Shea, who inspire me every day. —K.F.

For Michael, Mitch, and Olivia: Thank you for the domestic support, art direction (Liv), and for cheering me on. —J.C.D.

Special thanks to Mike Maher for his hard work and technical support.

A portion of the proceeds from every book sold will benefit
Ovations for the Cure of Ovarian Cancer. www.ovationsforthecure.org

It seems to me
that every day
I'm waiting for
my mom.

She's always
busy doing
things that take
so very long.

"Just one more minute,"
she often says, as I am standing by.
"I'm sick of being patient," I pout, trying not to cry.

If only Mom could do her tasks,
without me having to wait.
She'd tuck my sister in at night and read to me 'til late.

If I were
granted just
one wish,
I'd wish
to wait
no more.
I'd wish
that Mom
could play
with me
and still
complete
her chores.

An Octopus Named Mom
is what my wish would be!

No more playing games all by myself—now Mom could play with me!

It was a **blustery autumn** eve the night my wish was made.

The **moon** was bright; the wind was strong; the trees began to **sway**.

There was **something** in the air on that very chilly night.

It was then I knew the wish **I** made had started to **take flight.**

There she stood, my mother, yet she took a different form.
While her eyes and smile were just the same, her looks were not the norm.
Her skin was a soft color lilac with polka dots of blue....

She was **An Octopus Named Mom,**
and this was her big debut!
On all eight arms she came to me and scooped me from my bed.
She smiled, and she hugged me, then she kissed me on my head.

Her arms were aplenty, her cheeks like a rose.
A ruffled pink apron is what she wore for clothes.

Now that Mom
is an octopus,
I'm such a
happy boy.

She makes my bed
and combs my hair
while picking up my toys.

My mother is **amazing!** You should see what she **can** do! She can make my breakfast, bake us **treats**, and even tie my shoe.

She tends to every need I have; I never have to fuss.
She zips my coat and pats the dog
as we wait for the bus.

Life is **happy** and exciting.
We all have so much **fun!**

Now bath time turns to **playtime**, and her scrubbing still gets **done!**

When I awoke to the morning sun, things weren't as they had seemed.
The night's events had faded away; sadly, my wish was a dream.

But one thought did occur
to me, as I began to stir.
If I turned her into this octopus,
**my mother would
not be her.**

Her **beautiful** face, her loving **hugs** that feel so right to me—

Mom is perfect the way she is; she is just how she **should** be.

When she tucks me in at night, only her **two arms** will do.

So I better pray my mom stays put and my wish does **not** come true.

My mother wouldn't have to change if I could pitch in more.

I'm getting to be a **big** boy now; she could use **my help** for sure.

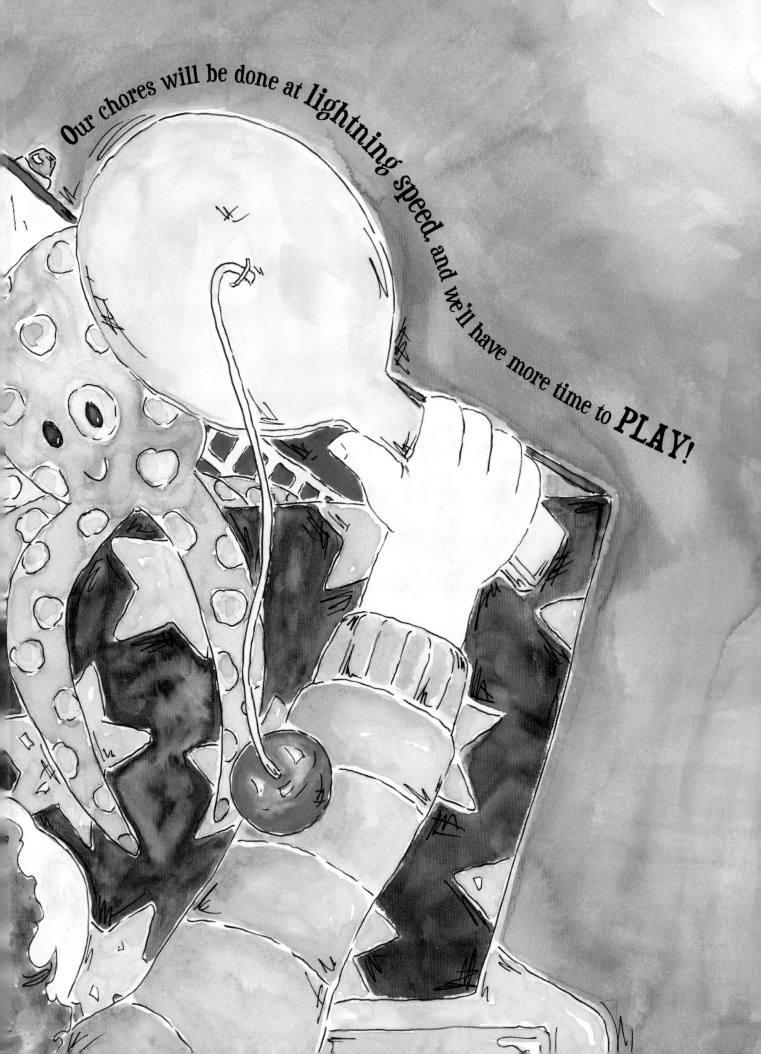

So Mother, when I wait for you and for all things to be done,

My wish for you is to stay like you, and I just like your son.